llama llama
gram and grandpa

Anna Dewdney

VIKING

Llama Llama, big big day!
It's a first—a special stay.

Pack up clothes and pj's tight—
Llama's going **overnight.**

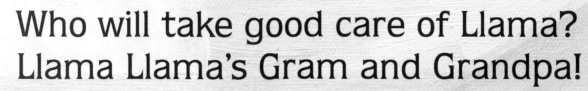

Who will take good care of Llama?
Llama Llama's Gram and Grandpa!

Bag and Fuzzy?
In the car!

Buckle up! The drive seems far. . . .

Hugs and kisses. Big hellos.

Mama loves you!

Off she goes.

A glass of milk. A yummy snack.

Now it's time to go unpack.

Mama's picture in a frame.
Different. Also **just the same.**

Take out socks
and pants
and book.

Put the jammies on the hook.

Feeling strange
away from Mama.

Llama dear, are you OK?

Llama doesn't want to say.

Grandma says,
Let's go outside.

Climb on up.
Pretend to ride.

Tractor, gardens, grass to mow—

Llama's having fun.
But . . . oh . . .

Fuzzy is still left at home.
Maybe Fuzzy feels **alone?**

Grandpa's workshop—lots to do.
Wood and hammers. Nails and glue.

Llama makes a little chair.

It's for Fuzzy . . .
who's **not there.**

Time for dinner. Help get ready.
Carry dishes. Hold them steady.

Grandma's house has different food.
Something squishy. Something *stewed*.

Llama tries it, and it's good.
Would you like more? Llama would!

Dinner's over. Time for bed.
Llama wants to wait, instead.

Grandpa says,
Let's see the stars.

Nighttime shows us where they are.

Take a bath.
Then comb and brush.

Settle in for stories. *Hush.*

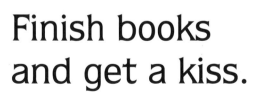

Finish books
and get a kiss.

Llama's lips begin to quiver.

Llama starts to shake and shiver.

Llama needs his Fuzzy near,

but FUZZY LLAMA ISN'T HERE!

Wait a minute.
Stay right here.

Grandpa leaves, then reappears.

When Grandpa was a little boy,
he also had a special toy.

Big or little, young or old,
a llama needs someone to hold.

A Grandma kiss.

A Grandpa hug.

Feeling cozy. Settled snug.

Llama Llama's not alone.

This *is* home . . .

away from home.

For grandparents everywhere, and the little llamas who love them.

VIKING
An Imprint of Penguin Random House LLC
375 Hudson Street
New York, New York 10014

First published in the United States of America by Viking, an imprint of Penguin Random House LLC, 2015

LIBRARY OF CONGRESS CATALOGING-IN-PUBLICATION DATA IS AVAILABLE
ISBN: 978-0-670-01396-8

Manufactured in China

1 3 5 7 9 10 8 6 4 2

Set in ITC Quorum Std

The art for this book was created with oil paint, colored pencil,
and oil pastel on primed canvas.